# alphabet Olympics

# ABC

Written by Michelle Stacey Sjodin

Illustrated by Andrew Zettler

For my sons, Nicholas and Jackson, the inspiration for this project - MSS


For my tiny loves Julia and Grace, and their passionate love of books - AZ

ISBN 978-0-9888065-1-1
Printed in the U.S.A
www.dearbabybooks.com

For inquiries to the Publisher, please email info@dearbabybooks.com

Alphabet Olympics
by Michelle Stacey Sjodin; illustrated by Andrew Zettler

Summary: Mastering the alphabet has never been so much fun. From Baseball Batting Badgers and Kickball Kangaroos to Ping Pong Playing Pumas and Zip-Lining Zebras, these fun and easy-to-remember mascots serve as memorable building blocks on the path to mastering letters and alphabet sounds.

**Written, illustrated, printed, and bound in the United States**

# Aa

## All-Star Archer Gators

Alex approaches archery with **awe-inspiring accuracy**. His **arrows achieve audience applause and accumulate awards** for his home team of **Alabama**.

# B b

## Brown Badgers

**Bubba** is a **bold batter** and a **bright base** runner from Beaumont.

This **badger brilliantly blasts baseballs** with his **bat!**

Did you know that Badgers are great diggers who live underground?

# Cc

## Canadian Curling Cats

**Charlie** and **Charlene captivate Canada's crowds** as they **competitively curl**. This **charming** duo is taking this **chilly** sport by storm. **Could** they be on their way to a **championship**?

# Dd

## Dodgeball Dinosaurs

**Dave** is a **dynamic dare-devil** from **Delaware**. He's a **diver** and a **dodger** who **ducks**, **defends**, and **drills dazzling dodgeballs** for his team.

**Don't doubt** these **dynamite Dinos**!

# Ee
## Excercising Elephants

Lead instructor **Elaine** will **educate** and **entertain** as she **exhibits** her **excellent excercises**! **Encino** will be sure to **enjoy** the **enormous efforts** of these **energetic elephants**!

Did you know that the elephant is the largest animal that lives on land!

# Ff

## Florida's Fabulous Flamingos

**Fiona** is a **fast-fetching flamingo**. She and her **friends** are in a **frenzy** for **frisbees**. They'll **face-off** and **fling** in a **flash** - that's a **fact**. These **flamingos** are sure to **facilitate fun** in the **Florida** sun!

# Gg

## Galloping Giraffes

This **gang** of **galloping giraffes** is led by **Gerald** and **Girard**. They **guard** and **get giveaways** with **gusto**. These **guys** are **geniuses** of their **Georgia gym** and are **guaranteed** to **gain gold**!

# Hh

## Handsome Hockey Hammerheads

Team captain **Harold heats** up the ice and is **happy** to **hit hard**. There will be no **half-hearted** or **haphazard hits** for these **half-crazed, headstrong hockey** loving **hammerheads** from **Harlem**!

How many H's can you count?

# I i

## Ice Skating Iguanas

**Ivonna is Iowa's ice** skating **iguana.** She **invents iconic ice** dances and **inspiring** spins. This **ice** skater **improvises impressively** on the **ice!**

I Love To Improvise!

# Jj

## Jumping Jaguars

**Jack Junior** is a **jovial jaguar** from **Jacksonville**. His **jaw-dropping jumps justify** grabbing gold!

# Kk

## The Kangaroos Of Kalamazoo

These **king-sized kickballers** are **keen** at **kicking**. **Kitty** will call you out when it's her turn at the plate - **KAPOW!**

# Ll

## Lacrosse Lions

**Louisville listens** for **Layne's lively laughter** while these **leaping lions launch lacrosse** balls **like lightning**. These **lovable lions** are **learning lacrosse** and **leaving** a **legacy**.

# Mm

## Motocrossing Monkeys

**Max** is a **mastermind** of **motocross**. He and his **medal-minded monkeys** have **managed many miles** over **Montana's mountains** with their **marvelous maneuvers**!

# Nn

## Netball Newts

These **nifty newts** from **Nevada** are **notorious** for **non-stop net** action. Playmaker **Nicholas navigates nimbly** and knows how to **neutralize** with a **nudge**. Soon they'll be **nationally** known as **number** one!

# Oo

## Oaring Octopi

Meet **Oscar** the **outstanding octopus** from **Oklahoma**. He's **on** an **oceanic** rowing **odyssey** with an **objective** to **outmaneuver** and **overtake** his competitors with high **octane!**

# Pp

## Ping-Ponging Pumas

Patricia **pounds** her **paddle** with **power** and **persistence** until she **perseveres** for her **Pennsylvanian** team. Her **purple paw** **packs** a **punch!**

# Qq

## Quoit Trowing Quails

These **quails** from **Queens** are **quick** to compete. Especially **Quentin**, when he concentrates on **quality**. He **quickly** makes the competition cringe & **quake**!

# Rr

## Racing Redbirds

**Robert's race** car is **really radical**. When he **revs** his **racing** engine and **rolls**, he **runs** the **Rhode** Island **racetrack** in first position for his **roaring** team.

# S s

## Shot-Putting Sasquatch

Meet **Sammy** the **shot-putting Sasquatch** from **Saratoga Springs**. His **stunning strength shatters** records with **surprising** ease.

# Tt

## Tennis Tasmanians

**Tony** is a **top tennis** player from **Texas**. He **tackles tennis** with **tenacity** and **terrific talent**. It's **totally trophy time!**

# U u

## Unicycling Urchins

**Uma** the **urchin** displays **unbelievable** balance **under** the sea. These **unusual unicycling Urchins** from **Utah** are **utterly** amazing as they ride on the **unique** and **unlevel** sea floor.

# Vv

## Volleyball Vipers

**Victor volleys** his way to **victory** with **veracity** & **vigor**. When these **varsity vipers** from **Virginia visit** the crowd is sure to get **very vocal**!

# Ww

## Water Polo Whales

Wally wobbles and wiggles through the water. Watch as he whips the ball into the goal. The wonders from Wisconsin will not settle for anything but a win.

# Xx

## X-Country Skier

**Xander** the cross-country skier knows exactly how to maximize his speed as he criss-crosses through the mountains on his freshly waxed skis!

# Yy

## The Yachting Yak

**Yaz yearns** to **yacht yearly** as far as he can go. If **you** ask him for a tour **you'll** surely enjoy the show.

# Zz

## Zip-Lining Zebra

**Zany Zack zigzags** though the air as he **zip-lines** over **Zimbabwe** with **zeal!**

CPSIA information can be obtained at www.ICGtesting.com
Printed in the USA
LVOW02*0610120214

373339LV00002BA/4/P